Ricky Ricotta's vs. the Uranium unicorns from Uranus

The Seventh Robot Adventure Novel by
DAV PILKEY
Pictures by
MARTIN ONTIVEROS

For Quaid and Will O'Brien
—D. P.

To Johnny Blaze, Syles, Mason, Nico, Zannabelle,
Evan, Stella, Pi, my new nephew Topoltzín, and
a special shout-out to Hazel Millie Spoons
—M. O.

Reg
SCHOLASTIC an(lastic Inc.

Th
auth(

ISBN 978 1407 10764 6

A CIP catalogue record for this book is available from the British Library.

Printed and bound by CPI Group (UK) Ltd, Croydon, CR0 4YY
Papers used by Scholastic Children's Books are made from wood grown in sustainable forests.

1 3 5 7 9 10 8 6 4 2

This is a work of fiction. Names, characters, places, incidents and dialogues are products
of the author's imagination or are used fictitiously. Any resemblance to actual people,
living or dead, events or locales is entirely coincidental.

www.scholastic.co.uk/zone
www.pilkey.com

Chapters

CHAPTER 1

Fun . . . and
Not Fun

One sunny morning, a little mouse
named Ricky Ricotta went out to
play with his giant mighty Robot.
    First, they came to the playground.

The mighty Robot pushed Ricky
on the swing set.

"This is fun," said Ricky.

Then Ricky tried to push his
Robot on the swing set.
"This is not fun," said Ricky.

Next, Ricky and his Robot flew to
the amusement park.

Ricky got on the Ferris wheel.

"This is fun!" said Ricky.

Then Ricky's mighty Robot got on
the Ferris wheel.

"This is not fun," said Ricky.

Finally, Ricky and his mighty
Robot went to the swimming pool.
Ricky did a perfect swan dive.
"That was fun!" said Ricky.

Then Ricky's Robot did a perfect
cannonball dive.
SPLASH!!!

"That was *NOT FUN*," said Ricky.

CHAPTER 2
The Wish

Ricky and his mighty Robot walked
home. Ricky was not happy.

That night after supper, Ricky's mighty Robot helped Ricky get ready for bed.

Usually Ricky enjoyed brushing
his teeth with the Turbo-Toothbrush
built into his Robot's pinky finger. . .

. . .but not tonight.

Usually Ricky laughed when his Robot helped him put on his pyjamas. . .

. . . but not tonight.

And usually Ricky had fun when
his Robot tucked him into bed. . .

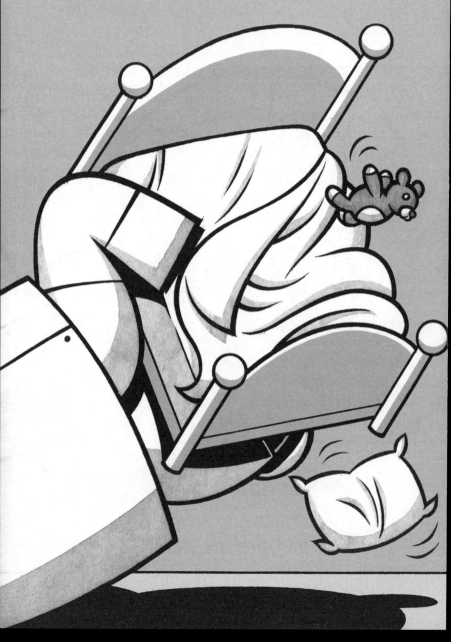

. . .but not tonight.

Ricky loved his mighty Robot, but sometimes it was hard having a best friend who was so *BIG*.

"I wish my mighty Robot had
somebody his own size to play
with," Ricky thought. "Then maybe
I could have fun by myself."

As Ricky went to sleep that
evening, he did not suspect that
his wish was about to come true.

CHAPTER 3

Uncle Unicorn

At that very moment, about 1,650 million kilometres away on a planet called Uranus, a nasty creature named Uncle Unicorn was hatching a hideous plan.

Uncle Unicorn was the president of Unicorp Inc. He had made a lot of money by turning his planet into a nuclear dumping ground.

All over the galaxy, creatures came to unload their toxic waste on to Uranus.

Most of the unicorns who lived on Uranus had moved away a long time ago. But the three who remained had mutated into gigantic Uranium Unicorns, and they served their evil boss with glee.

That night, Uncle Unicorn looked out at his planet through the window of his tall office building.

"I've destroyed my entire planet," he laughed. "Now I shall take over the Earth."

Uncle Unicorn knew about Ricky's mighty Robot. He knew that the evilest minds in the galaxy had tried to fight Ricky's Robot and failed.

"But I've got a trick that's SURE to stop Ricky Ricotta's mighty Robot once and for all!" snarled Uncle Unicorn.

TO: MIGHTY ROBOT

Uncle Unicorn took his three Uranium Unicorns into his rocket ship and blasted off towards Earth.

CHAPTER 4
The Ladybot

The next day, Ricky ran out to the garage where his mighty Robot slept.

"Mighty Robot!" cried Ricky. "You got a present! You got a present!"

Ricky's Robot threw off his pyjamas and ran to see the giant present.

"I wonder who it is from?" asked Ricky.

Ricky's mighty Robot opened up
the present.

Inside was a giant Ladybot.

She was big and silver, and she
had a giant heart on her chest.

Suddenly, the giant heart opened up and a laser beam shot out. It zapped Ricky's Robot right in his eyes.

"Hey!" shouted Ricky. "What's the big idea?"

The giant heart closed back up again, and the Ladybot returned to normal. But Ricky's mighty Robot was not normal any more. He had changed. He had a funny look in his eyes. He was *in LOVE*!

The Ladybot held out her hand,
and Ricky's mighty Robot took it.
Then, together, the two Robots turned
and skipped away down the street.
BOOM! BOOM! BOOM!
"Mighty Robot!" called Ricky.
"Come back here!"
But Ricky's mighty Robot was gone.

CHAPTER 5

Alone

Ricky tried to follow his mighty
Robot, but he could not keep up.
"Hey, wait for me!" Ricky called.
But the two Robots did not wait.
Ricky was all alone.

That night, Ricky's mighty Robot
did not come home for supper.

He was not there to help Ricky
brush his teeth. . .

. . .or put on his pyjamas. . .

. . .or tuck him into bed.

"Would you like us to tuck you
in tonight?" asked Ricky's parents.

"No, thank you," said Ricky.

And he went to sleep with a
sad heart.

CHAPTER 6
The Next Day

The next day, Ricky went looking for his mighty Robot. He searched all over town, but he could not find his Robot anywhere.

Then Ricky hiked into the woods.
Deep inside the forest, Ricky
finally found his mighty Robot.
But as he got closer, Ricky
discovered something horrible.

Ricky's mighty Robot had been chained to a giant rocket ship. The mighty Robot was surrounded by three evil Uranium Unicorns. And it looked as if *everyone* was under the horrible spell of. . .

. . .the Ladybot.

"A-*HA*!" said Ricky. "I *KNEW* that Ladybot was up to no good!"

Suddenly, the Ladybot's giant heart opened up, and Uncle Unicorn peeked out.

"Now that we've got that mighty Robot under the spell of our evil Hypno-Ray," said Uncle Unicorn, "he won't be able to stop our terrible plans! But just to be on the safe side, I want you Uranium Unicorns to DESTROY him!"

"OH, NO!" gasped Ricky. "I've got to save my mighty Robot!"

CHAPTER 7

Help Is on the Way

Ricky ran back through the woods and all the way to the other side of town. Finally, he reached his cousin Lucy's house.

Lucy was in the backyard playing with her three pet Jurassic Jackrabbits, Fudgie, Cupcake, and Waffles.

"Hi, Ricky," said Lucy. "Do you want to play *princess*?"

"NO!" cried Ricky, panting hard and out of breath. "I . . . NEED . . . TO . . . BORROW . . . WAFFLES!"

"Come on, Waffles," said Lucy.
"This looks like an emergency!"
Lucy and Ricky climbed on to
Waffles's back and prepared
for takeoff.

Fudgie and Cupcake wanted to help, too, but Lucy told them to stay home.

"You guys are too clumsy to be helpful," said Lucy. "Just stay here and guard the cookies!"

And with a flap of Waffles's wings, the three friends took off into the sky.

CHAPTER 8
Inside the Ladybot

Soon, Ricky, Lucy, and Waffles
reached the woods. There they saw
Ricky's mighty Robot being held
by the Uranium Unicorns.

"My mighty Robot has been hypnotized," said Ricky. "And those evil Unicorn guys are going to destroy him!"

"But what can we do?" asked Lucy.

"We've got to stop that giant Ladybot now!" said Ricky. "She's controlling my Robot with a Hypno-Ray!"

Waffles landed carefully on the Ladybot's shoulder.

Ricky and Lucy climbed into the Ladybot's ear and looked around for a way to turn off the Hypno-Ray.

Suddenly, Uncle Unicorn found
Ricky and Lucy.

"So, you thought you could save
the day, huh?" laughed Uncle
Unicorn. "Well, you were WRONG!"
Uncle Unicorn tied up Ricky and
Lucy and hung them high above the
main generator.

Ricky looked down at the generator.
"If only there were some way I
could destroy that generator," said
Ricky. "But how?"

CHAPTER 9

The Generator

Just then, a few drops of sweat dripped from Ricky's face. They fell down into the generator. Suddenly, a giant spark flashed out of the generator, followed by a puff of black smoke. The generator stopped for a split second, then continued running.

"A-*HA*!" cried Ricky. "If I can get
that generator wet, it will shut down!"

Ricky tried to sweat more, but he
couldn't. He tried to spit into the
generator, but his mouth was too dry.

"Lucy," said Ricky. "You've got to spit down on to that generator!"

"No way!" said Lucy. "Princesses do *NOT* spit!"

"Pleeeeease?" Ricky begged. "It's a matter of life and death!" But Lucy still refused.

Then, Ricky got a sneaky idea.

"Just think," said Ricky. "If those Unicorns destroy the planet, there will be no more ice cream and no more chocolate-chip cookies. . . "

"N-n-no more ice cream?" Lucy whimpered. Her eyes welled up with tears. "N-n-no more chocolate-chip cookies?"

Giant teardrops began dripping
down Lucy's face.

"And no more candy floss and
coconut cream pie," said Ricky.
"And no more vanilla wafers and
grape lollipops."

"N-n-no more g-g-grape lollipops?"
cried Lucy.

Suddenly, Lucy burst into tears. Giant tears sprayed from her face and fell down into the generator below.

Bright sparks and horrible black smoke began shooting out of the generator. It shook back and forth. Then, finally, it broke down.

"Hooray!" shouted Ricky.

CHAPTER 10
Ricky's Robot Returns

The generator was broken, the Ladybot had shut down, and the Hypno-Ray had stopped working. Suddenly, Ricky's mighty Robot returned to normal.

The mighty Robot did not know
where he was, or what was going on,
but he knew he had to save the day.

With a mighty burst of Robo-Power,
Ricky's Robot snapped his chains.
Then, they all started to fight.

The big, bad beasties banded
together and butted the Robot's behind.

So Ricky's Robot unleashed an
ultra-unbeatable Unicorn uppercut.

Then the plucky protector prevailed by punching the putrid ponies into a perilous pile-up.

The Uranium Unicorns were very angry.

"No more horsing around," they said. "It's time to kick some Robot tushy!"

CHAPTER 11

The Big Battle
(in FLIP-O-RAMA™)

STEP 1

Place your *left* hand inside the dotted lines marked "LEFT HAND HERE." Hold the book open *flat*.

STEP 2

Grasp the *right-hand* page with your right thumb and index finger (inside the dotted lines marked "RIGHT THUMB HERE").

STEP 3

Now *quickly* flip the right-hand page back and forth until the picture appears to be *animated*.

(For extra fun, try adding your own sound effects!)

FLIP-O-RAMA 1

(pages 77 and 79)

Remember, flip *only* page 77.
While you are flipping, make sure
you can see the picture on page 77
and the one on page 79.
If you flip quickly, the two
pictures will start to look like
<u>one</u> *animated* picture.

Don't forget to add
your own sound effects!

LEFT HAND HERE

The Uranium Unicorns
Attacked.

RIGHT
THUMB
HERE

The Uranium Unicorns
Attacked.

FLIP-O-RAMA 2

(pages 81 and 83)

Remember, flip *only* page 81.
While you are flipping, make sure
you can see the picture on page 81
and the one on page 83.
If you flip quickly, the two
pictures will start to look like
<u>one</u> *animated* picture.

Don't forget to add
your own sound effects!

LEFT HAND HERE

Ricky's Mighty Robot
Fought Back.

RIGHT
THUMB
HERE

Ricky's Mighty Robot
Fought Back.

FLIP-O-RAMA 3

(pages 85 and 87)

Remember, flip *only* page 85.
While you are flipping, make sure
you can see the picture on page 85
and the one on page 87.
If you flip quickly, the two
pictures will start to look like
<u>one</u> *animated* picture.

Don't forget to add
your own sound effects!

LEFT HAND HERE

The Uranium Unicorns
Battled Hard.

RIGHT
THUMB
HERE

The Uranium Unicorns
Battled Hard.

FLIP-O-RAMA 4

(pages 89 and 91)

Remember, flip *only* page 89.
While you are flipping, make sure
you can see the picture on page 89
and the one on page 91.
If you flip quickly, the two
pictures will start to look like
<u>one</u> *animated* picture.

Don't forget to add
your own sound effects!

LEFT HAND HERE

Ricky's Mighty Robot
Battled Harder.

89

RIGHT
THUMB
HERE

Ricky's Mighty Robot
Battled Harder.

FLIP-O-RAMA 5

(pages 93 and 95)

Remember, flip *only* page 93.
While you are flipping, make sure
you can see the picture on page 93
and the one on page 95.
If you flip quickly, the two
pictures will start to look like
<u>one</u> *animated* picture.

Don't forget to add
your own sound effects!

LEFT HAND HERE

Ricky's Mighty Robot
Won the War.

RIGHT
THUMB
HERE

Ricky's Mighty Robot
Won the War.

CHAPTER 12

The Super Mecha-Evil Ladybot

Ricky's mighty Robot had defeated the Uranium Unicorns, but Uncle Unicorn was not ready to give up just yet.

Quickly, he turned on the backup generator, and then he pressed a secret button on his control panel.

SECRET BUTTON

Suddenly, the Ladybot
began to grow. . .

. . .until she was as big as a mountain
and as deadly as a million volcanoes.

The gigantic Ladybot took one
horrible step. . .

Ricky and Lucy untied their ropes
and ran out of the Ladybot's ear.
Uncle Unicorn chased after them. . .

. . .but Ricky's mighty Robot
stopped him just in time.

"My beautiful Ladybot is
destroyed!" cried Uncle Unicorn.
"How did it happen?"

"It looks like somebody tied her
shoelaces together," said Ricky.

"But who could have done that?"
asked Lucy.

Just then, Fudgie and Cupcake
poked their heads out of the bushes.
They had been helpful after all.

"Hooray for Fudgie and Cupcake!"
cried Lucy.

CHAPTER 13
Justice Prevails

Ricky's Mighty Robot stuffed the three
Uranium Unicorns into their rocket
ship and threw it back to Uranus.

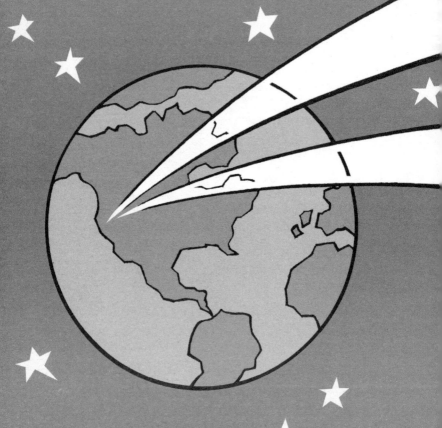

Then, he picked up the giant
Ladybot and threw her back, too.

Finally, they all took Uncle
Unicorn to the Squeakyville Jail.
"Hey, this place is getting
crowded!" shouted Uncle Unicorn.

Ricky and his mighty Robot flew Lucy and her Jurassic Jackrabbits back to their house.

"Do you want to stay and play *princess*?" asked Lucy.

"No, thanks," said Ricky. "I've got something important to do!"

And, together, the two friends flew home.

CHAPTER 14

Bedtime

That night after supper, Ricky helped his mighty Robot get ready for bed.

Ricky brushed his Mighty Robot's giant teeth. . .

. . .then he helped his Mighty Robot put on his pyjamas. . .

. . .and, finally, he tucked his mighty Robot into bed.

"I'm glad you boys are having fun
again," said Ricky's father, "even
though you are both very different."

"Me, too," said Ricky. . .

HOW TO DRAW RICKY

1.

2.

3.

4.

5.

6.

7.

8.

9.

10.

11.

12.

HOW TO DRAW RICKY'S ROBOT

1.

2.

3.

4.

5.

6.

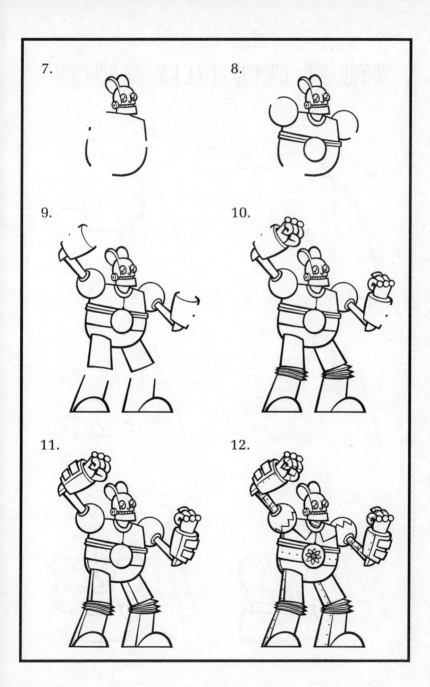

HOW TO DRAW UNCLE UNICORN

1.

2.

3.

4.

5.

6.

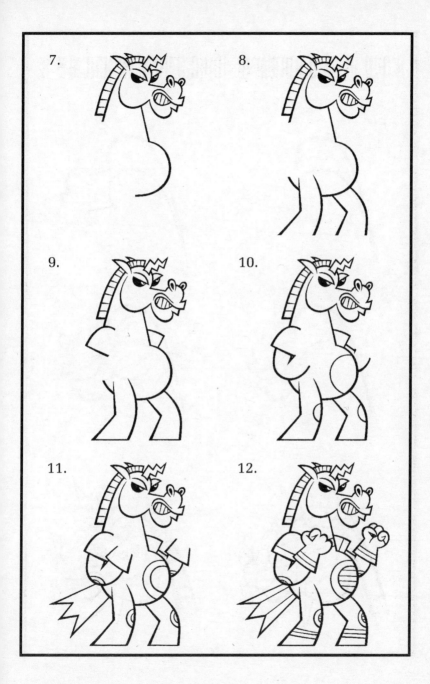

121

HOW TO DRAW A URANIUM UNICORN

1.

2.

3.

4.

5.

6.

123

HOW TO DRAW THE LADYBOT

1.

2.

3.

4.

5.

6.

124

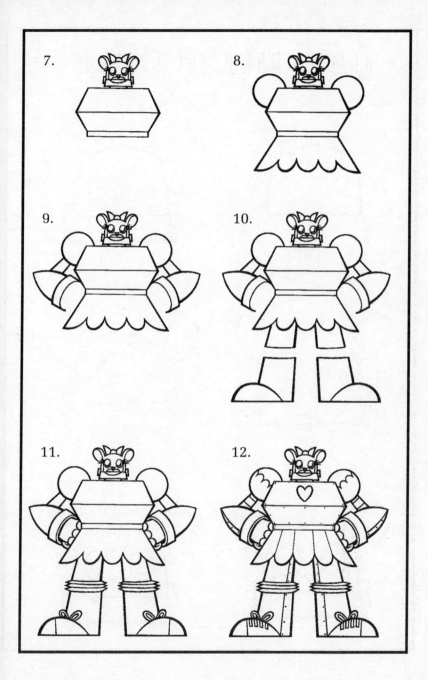

About the Author and Illustrator

DAV PILKEY created his first stories as comic books while he was in elementary school. In 1997, he wrote and illustrated his first adventure novel for children, *The Adventures of Captain Underpants*, which received rave reviews and was an instant bestseller – as were all the books that followed in the series. Dav is also the creator of numerous award-winning picture books. He and his dog live in Eugene, Oregon.

It was a stroke of luck when Dav discovered the work of artist **MARTIN ONTIVEROS**. Dav knew that Martin was just the right illustrator for the *Ricky Ricotta's Mighty Robot* series. Martin has loved drawing since he was a kid. He lives in Portland, Oregon. He has a lot of toys, which he shares with his young son, Felix.